HISTORICAL SEX COLLECTION

EXPLICIT DIRTY EROTICA SHORT STORIES

KELLIE GRANIER

plicit Press
Erotica Fiction

CHAPTER 1

AFTERNOON TRYST

I WAS A TYPICAL VICTORIAN LADY. I loved dressing beautifully, decorating my house with floral designs and unique artwork, and enjoying afternoon tea with my friends. Today I had planned a tea with a rather unusual person. I usually invited other ladies from my community, but today an unorthodox guest was coming to my parlor for tea and crumpets. I had invited a gentleman to join me. He was an intellectual, a writer of sorts. He had joined our small community a few months ago and I found him interesting since the day I met him. Yes, I was married and I will admit I invited him to join me at a time I knew my husband would be gone. I will also admit I had a bit of a crush on this gentleman, Mr. Newberry, but only I was aware of this.

I readied myself for his arrival. I put my hair up in a beautiful French twist and wore a lovely scarlet-colored corset with a long satin black skirt. I put on a bit of rouge and lipstick in the palest of pink and a spritz or two of a floral fragrance for behind my ears. I knew in my heart that I desired to seduce Mr. Newberry, but I hoped it wasn't too obvious.

I heard the bell so I raced through the parlor to the foyer and opened the door. There was Mr. Newberry. "Hello, Mr. Newberry. Welcome. Please come inside." I said as I took his overcoat.

"Please call me Richard." He replied as he followed me inside.

Richard and I had a nice chat and talked about many things. He was so interesting and it just made me want him more. As he was talking I couldn't help but notice how handsome he was. He had a chiseled jaw and beautiful dark green eyes. The way he looked at me with them was very seductive. As he talked I could see him look me over and examine my features. I also noticed he paused a moment when he looked at my ample breasts. I could feel the sexual tension building in the air. It was apparent he and I were attracted to one another and it was a desire that we would not be able to contain much longer.

I felt a bit uncomfortable with the sexual tones hanging over us and I shifted in my seat. I was a married woman but I was having trouble controlling my carnal desires. I usually wasn't like this but Richard was getting under my skin unlike any other man had ever gotten under my skin. I was wondering how I should handle the growing feelings of erotic desire and the wetness that was forming underneath my skirt when Richard surprised me by scooting closer to me on the sofa. He took his hand and caressed my left breast and that's all it took. We suddenly found ourselves embroiled in a passionate and wet kiss.

Once we started to kiss I knew I wasn't going to stop and that we were going to go all the way with our encounter. In other words, I knew that Richard and I were going to make love and do everything sexual we had on our minds.

CHAPTER 2

CABIN IN THE WOODS

MY HUSBAND HAD BEEN GONE for so long now I had finally decided he must be dead out in the wilderness of North Dakota. It was hard for me to come to terms with it. I got lonely out here alone by myself with no one to talk to. Occasionally I would ride my horse into town and buy my essentials and sell my vegetables from the garden. My husband left over 3 months ago to find better work and hopefully provide a better life for us. He and I both knew that it was a risk he was taking, and he may not come back. I struggled to accept the truth but I finally had to force myself to.

Tonight I had just settled in for the evening with a good book in hand. I had lit the oil lamps and warmed the cabin well. I was just about to drift off into a peaceful sleep when I heard my bloodhound barking on the porch of my cabin. My first thought was maybe my husband was returning but I knew not to get too excited about that. It was probably just a raccoon or deer outside that my dog Jake had seen or smelled.

I got my oil lamp and went outside on the porch to take

a look, and I was startled to see a man about 20 yards away. I looked at him with shock, fear, and a bit of curiosity. Then he spoke and said, "Ma'am I am sorry to have startled you. I don't mean you any harm. I have been traveling by horseback for two days and I am so tired. Would it be possible for me to come inside and rest a bit and maybe get something to drink?" I looked him over a bit suspiciously and decided his face looked honest enough. I usually had a pretty good intuition about people and he seemed like a truthful person, so I decided to go ahead and let the poor guy come inside to rest.

"Can I get you some coffee or water, maybe a bowl of homemade soup?" I asked the stranger politely.

"Yes ma'am, that would be wonderful. Thank you very much." He said with appreciation in his voice.

I told him to sit down and make himself comfortable. I prepared the traveler a warm bowl of my soup and got him a hearty slice of cornbread. As I spooned the soup into the bowl I couldn't help but notice his virile and masculine form. His hands were big and powerful looking and he had thick fingers like he had done hard labor. That was really a turn-on for me and caused me to feel a bit tingly all over my flesh.

It had been months since I had the strong arms of a man around me. My mind took me back to the incredible feelings. How my body longed for his touch and I could taste the kisses of desire as he made his way from my breasts up to my lips. I got lost in my fantasy and then noticed my visitor was speaking to me. He was asking if he could go to my bath area and clean up. I told him sure. I gave him some towels and heard him inside bathing. I must admit I was dying to sneak a peek at him. I couldn't resist so I looked through the small crack at him. He was amazingly handsome and his cock was big and round. It made me feel a familiar stir inside my groin area; I hadn't been made love to in so long., I was literally aching. He dried his shaft off and pulled it slowly with his towel I swear I let out an audible "mmmmmm" that I am sure he heard, but I didn't care. I was so horny I was almost ready to jump his body. I went and lay down on my cot and began to run my fingers through my drenched snatch. It was so wet I could hardly finger my pussy. My hand kept slipping off. I pulled out one of my tits and started to lick the extremely hard nipple as the smell of lavender wafted through the air from his bath. I was so into what I was doing that I didn't notice him watching me. But I heard a noise and looked up to see him jerking on his very hard rod slowly and sexily. I continued to play with my furry pussy and spread my legs open so he could see my girly bits.

He came over and began to ravage between my legs, eating my pussy as if he had never eaten a pussy before. I yelped in delight. It had been ages since I had been eaten off this good. I had masturbated but never been able to eat the fuck out of myself. He reached up with his hands and ripped my snaps to my corset wide open revealing my plum juice tits. They were very large and nearly pulsating for him to partake of them. He slid his manly form on top of me and began to lap and lick my tits until they hurt, but it felt so erotic I didn't care. The idea of being taken by a stranger was so erotic and taboo it made me seethe with want and need.

I yanked his mouth to me and began to kiss him like a wild and starved beast. I licked and lapped and our tongues warred at the other's, vying for the wet attention. He slid his girth inside of my hole inch by inch and I winced in red hot pleasure. It had been months since a man had fucked me and I was starving for it. He fucked me so hard and animal-like I began to scream out loud and he groaned like a raging lion. We started to cum in perfect unison as my fingernails groped down his back drawing blood and he screamed an animal sound that rang out through the woods I am sure. We both collapsed into a satisfied heap onto my cot. I awoke the next morning and he was nowhere to be found, but I will always remember the handsome stranger in my cabin in the woods and I long for the day he returns to fill my sexual desires and needs.

CHAPTER 3

DAUGHTER OF THE GREEK GOD

PRINCESS LEAH PRANCED BACK and forth in her room. Her heart was heavy and her pain and sadness were bewildering. Today was the day before the tournament. Her father was the Concord, the God. Concord was the Greek God who ruled over their lands. As the daughter of God, she was required to remain pure and untouched. To her, that almost seemed like a burden. Her father ruled with an iron fist and defying his wishes would only lead to one thing, complete peril. And so, although her heart belonged to Simon, the young gladiator, her body and her loyalty remained true to her family.

As she stepped out of the temple, she could see the people below busily conducting business in the market. "My Lady, there's a lad here to see you." Her faithful servant Nina informed. As she turned around slowly, the sight of Simon caught her eyes. He was well dressed in his armor as if he were about to go to war. "I just came by to bid you farewell, my dear princess."

"Simon...Why?" she asked. Her eyes grew dark with concern, as curiosity lingered upon her gorgeous features

"I have no other choice, your highness," his voice was soft and husky.

"Leave us at once," she commanded. The other people in the room with them immediately obeyed her order without hesitating. Once they were alone, she approached him steadily.

"Tell me, my love, who is the best warrior in all the land?"

"I am, my lady," he replied solemnly. He didn't look at her, instead, his head was down, and he spoke with an unconvincing tone.

"Why then do you doubt your strength? Why do you fear my love? You're the bravest warrior in all this land. Fear not, you will defeat Majored," she said cupping his face in her hand. As she brought her lips to his, her body arched for his. She desired nothing more than to comfort her dear lover, to let him know that everything would be okay. His lean muscular body against hers made her desire to be in his arms forever even greater. Taking his lips with much urgency and passion, she swept him off his feet with her desire.

He didn't give a bit of resistance. His kisses proved to be just as hunger-filled as hers. As they kissed, he began stroking her gorgeous long legs, working his way upwards beneath her gown. When his long fingers found her moist core, she yelped as he slipped two of his fingers into her slit. Pulling his fingers out slowly, he brought them to her lips and asked her to taste her sweet juices.

Princess Leah immediately parted her lips and took his

fingers into her mouth sucking it hard. Simon groaned in ecstasy as spasms shot through his body. She immediately took him into her mouth once again and sucked harder. Desires rocked her entire body as his tongue explored the insides of her mouth.

As their kisses intensified, they began ripping away each other's clothing, their bodies overcome with desire. Once she was completely naked Simon stepped aside to take in her full nakedness.

She looked amazing. Her soft lily-white skin was warm and delicious. He stroked her flesh with his tongue. As he took her into his mouth, moans of pleasure coursed through her body. His delicious tongue on her bare skin felt amazing. Leah let out several soft moans as he continued to caress her nipples.

Leah threw her head backward and let out several sharp cries. She could feel her juices slowly trickling down her inner thighs. Simon scooped her up in his strong masculine arms and carried her over to the bed. Once there, he propped her onto the soft bed and parted her legs gently. As his tongue made contact with her flesh.

Leah squirmed a little. He was bringing about an unimaginable amount of pleasure. His tongue lapped out her juices as he flicked it up and down her tenderness. Her fingers dug into the stain sheets for support as sensations gripped her body. Simon moved his tongue onwards to her throbbing clitoris.

Biting it gently, he increased her pleasure

"Oh, God. Don't stop Simon," she beckoned her voice thick with desire. Simon did everything he could to bring her closer to her climax. Her body seemed to spiral out of control when he began darting his tongue feverishly into her wetness. Over and over, he flicked his tongue in and out of her slit. Finally, with a loud cry, Princess Leah submitted to her earth-shattering climax. Simon wasted no time and soon he'd positioned himself between her legs. He pressed his huge cock against the tender flesh of her pussy as it made its way down into her delicious slit. Her juices seemed to coat his cock as he began working his way in and out of her wetness. Severing her with a series of long hard thrusts followed by shorter quicker thrusts. His panting became heavier and louder as he went along. Soon he was penetrating her core relentlessly. Each hard thrust that he gave made her pussy quiver. Her juices slowly trickled down her folds as she creamed his cock with her wetness. The room was soon filled with their loud moaning and groaning and soon he increased his momentum tremendously. His shaft rammed into her core as he buried himself to the held inside her. Her tightness hugged his cock as it rammed into her pussy with fury.

He pulled out briefly and brought his tongue back to her pussy. Her temple of delight tasted even better now that he'd been inside her. As he continued caressing her sensitive bud, she let out several loud cries. He ended his little torture and penetrated her wetness with his massive shaft once again. Her body jerked forward as he continued to scuff her heated core with his raw meat. Her loud moans were soon muffled by his hungry desire filled lips. As he kissed her passionately, he increased the momentum of his thrusts. Her fingers stroked his back.

A jolt of pleasure seemed to rock her body with each of his hard powerful thrusts. Over and over Simon buried himself, inside her. Finally, he let out a loud thunderous groan, which was coupled with several hard mighty thrusts.

His hot juices exploded inside her. At that same time, Princess Leah also let out a loud ecstatic cry as she too reached yet another amazingly delicious climax. He remained inside her for a while, exhausted and spent. He then pulled his cock and stroked it a few times with his hand, spilling his juices on her stomach. She gave him an exhausted smile.

CHAPTER 4

HER RUNAWAY LOVER

"THOSE PLANTATION WORKERS ARE SURE HARD-WORKING." Elizabeth turned around from the window where she had been gazing out into the open tobacco plantation. A few inches away from her stood Madeline, one of her domestic helpers. Madeline was one of three helpers she had that was assigned to cater to her every need, by her father Sir Ronald Fixworth, of York.

Elizabeth Fixworth had moved to the New World with her family at the tender age of five.

Now twenty years later, they owned one of the largest tobacco plantations in Virginia, with hundreds of men working the fields.

The word "slaves" did something to her heart, and she rather not even say it. She opposed what her family did, and if she could have her way, she'd free all the workers. She had been looking out into the fields admiring Meacham, one of the young plantation workers. For some time now, she'd been attracted to Meacham, but because of the difference in their social class, she feared the repercussions of declaring her love for him. The two of them had been secretly meeting and seeing each other. She didn't fear for herself, but instead for him. Her father Sir Fixworth would have his head and feed it to the dogs if he'd ever even caught them in a compromising position. However, her desire for him only grew as time went on. She often fantasized about the two of them making love, his body grinding against hers as the sweat from their passion trickled down from his lean body unto hers.

Physically speaking Meacham was a very attractive man; tall, dark, with a strong masculine frame, rising to about 6 feet 2 inches. He had a deep mysterious look, one of pain and anguish. She'd always wished she could take away his pain – soothe his mind. In her conversations with Madeline, she'd found out that he'd been captured while out hunting. His family had been left behind in the small village on the coast of Africa where he was originally from.

"I love Meacham and I want to be with him," she admitted to Madeline who was standing behind her.

"Miss Elizabeth are you sure you want to do that?" she had a genuine look of concern in her eyes. She knew all too well that the plantation workers weren't allowed to associate with the plantation owners or their families.

"I don't really care what my father thinks at this point Madeline," She huffed as she strode across the room, to her journal.

"Dear Journal,

Yet another excruciating day without the man I love. My heart bleeds for him, but I am comforted by the thought of our future plans. At full moon tonight, we will set forth on our journey to freedom. Freedom for him and me both."

. . .

The door opened and she quickly hid her journal in the drawer of her dresser. Her father stood in her doorway, with a few documents in hand. "I brought these for you, your tutor will be coming in late today...He has requested that you get started with these." He propped the stack of papers before her and stood in his usual uptight manner. The serious look on his face indicated, that he wanted to see her going through the documents in his presence.

Elizabeth absolutely hated how her father tried to dominate her life, almost as if she were one of his servants. "I'll get to it, in a minute," She gave him a reassuring smile, as she picked up her hairbrush and combed through her silky blonde hair.

"No you will get to it now!" her father yanked the brush from her hand and tossed it to the side.

Elizabeth said nothing to him, but in her mind, she knew this would be the last time he ever treated her as if she meant nothing to him. In her mind, she knew that when she and Meacham ran away tonight her father would regret all his unkindness towards her. And so, she pretended to go through the stacks of papers and books to appease him. He soon left and allowed her to continue her studies privately.

Before long night came, and as she peered through the tiny crack in her bedroom door she could see all the lights being turned off. It was time. She crept over to her bedroom window and quietly pushed it open. Her eyes perused the exterior of her house to ensure that no one was watching. Elizabeth fully slid through the window and made her way to the secret spot at the back of the plantation house where she had planned to meet her lover.

Meacham was already there waiting, looking as handsome as ever. Without too much hesitation, they rushed through the plantation, until they reached the secret underground tunnel that he'd dug. As they made their escape, their hearts pounded with fear. If they were caught, they would both be punished severely. Finally, they made it to the other side of the plantation. As they rushed away into the nearby bushes, they didn't stop running until the sun came up in the morning. At the bridge ahead, they could see Mr. Hemsorth, her tutor. He'd agreed to help them out, saying that the truly educated people were not in favor of slavery.

He had two horses with him. They greeted each other before straddling the horses and riding off with Mr. Hemsorth in the lead. Finally, they made it to a secluded area. "You'll be safe here," he said to them, as he led them to the small hut, hidden behind some bushes. They were a good distance from her house; in fact, they were, far away from her house.

They spent the day together, the three of them, before Mr. Hemsorth finally left them, telling them he was less than a mile away if they needed anything. That evening Elizabeth and Meacham celebrated their escape next to a small fire that kept them warm.

"We did it!" She exclaimed her voice laced with excitement. In that moment she launched across to where he sat and he caught her in his strong masculine arms.

"I know, the Gods have listened to us and answered our prayers." he cupped her chin in his hand and planted a soft passionate kiss on her lips. Before long, his tongue was viciously exploring the insides of her mouth demanding her sweet surrender. Her body quivered as he continued to kiss her with his hunger-filled lips.

His kisses finally left her lips and trailed downwards towards the nape of her gorgeous long neck. She purred as he sucked hard onto her tender flesh, causing tiny spasms to shoot through her body. His tongue felt warm and amazingly delicious as it stroked her skin.

Slowly he ripped her clothing away until she was completely naked before him. He pulled away for a brief minute and admired her gorgeous body. Elizabeth was by far the most beautiful maiden he'd ever laid eyes upon.

"You're so beautiful." His eyes carefully scrutinized her body inch by inch.

His words made her more away of her nakedness, but surprisingly she was also more aroused; she now wanted him completely naked himself. Changing positions with him, quickly she brought her kisses down to his groin. As she whipped out his long, hard cock, she let out a loud groan.

Her tongue immediately began working his shaft. She was licking and sucking it feverishly. His body stiffened as sensations rushed through his entire being. The way she moved her tongue over and around the head of his cock sent waves of pleasure through his body. Gripping the base of his cock firmly with her closed fist, she tried to take the entire cock into her mouth, but she couldn't; he was too well endowed to be swallowed with one mouthful.

Pulling her lips away from him, he eased her body down unto the bare earth, her hair fanning across the ground around her face. She looked simply divine. With his cock in his hand, he stroked it to the degree of erection that he wanted, before lowering himself unto her.

Elizabeth parted her legs, allowing him entry into her temple of delight. Her body yelped as his massive cock stroked her tender folds, and made its way to her warm core. Slowly he penetrated the slit of her pussy with his manhood. Her body tensed up as she closed her eyes and dug into the bare earth with her fingers. The feel of his massive rock-hard shaft, penetrating moist heat was almost unbearably delicious. With one hard thrust, he buried himself fully into her warmness.

"Oh God, yes!" She moaned breathlessly, as he began moving in and out of her wet pussy. His cock ramming against the walls of her pussy with each hard thrust. Meacham was groaning loudly and panting heavily as he continued to serve her with a series of long hard thrusts followed by shorter quicker thrusts.

Wave after wave of pleasure came coursing through her body, as he brought her closer to her earth-shattering climax.

Finally, with a loud groan and mighty hard thrust, they both summated their amazing climax.

Their juices oozed out of her pussy and unto the bare ground.

His gaze fell into hers, and a look of love and devotion filled his eyes. He was hers now and forever, free from all the norms and restrictions of the society that they lived in. He was her runaway lover.

CHAPTER 5

LYING WITH THE KING (THE KING IN ME)

SHE COULDN'T KNOW that under the mess on the bed the king still lay sleeping. After all, despite his size and his brutish manner in waking life, the burly beast slept silently. So when Leah, half the king's age and a third his size, pulls the covers from the bed, she is more than a little surprised to find that underneath it all the king is asleep, naked. The rush of cold over his body wakes him immediately, both of them looking at the king's massive cock before they look at each other's faces.

The king isn't embarrassed, pleased instead that there is cunt within arm's reach. His hands are on his chambermaid quickly, his eyes a mix of lust and fire that offers the delicate Leah little assurance. She's in his arms, smelling the spicy fragrances coming off his skin. The king is hairy, and his hair despite its mass, is soft. The black curls brush against Leah gently and she lets her arms go around the king as he kisses her. His kiss isn't gentle though, his cock needing to be dealt with. And that he won't be taking his cock in his own hands this morning has the royal scepter throbbing.

Leah's skirt is lifted, her undergarment also. The fabric is just above her waist now, her cunt exposed, and her back flat on the bed. There is no more kissing as the king's erection is suddenly dangling dangerously above her pussy. She knows that his majesty doesn't know her name. She doesn't care. She cares only that once this is done she will forever know that she was fucked by the most powerful man in the world, in her world. This will make bearable whatever second-rate servant she might be cursed to marry later. So despite her dry cunt, and her total lack of preparation for this unexpected early morning fuck, she is not going to make it hard for the king.

She lifts her legs and moves them apart so that her cunt is as open as it can be without her actually prying it apart with her own fingers. The king's hands are on her thighs, then his fingers are on her cunt. He sends one finger into the space, realizing the dryness. This isn't a terrain he can send his thick cock into comfortably. He wants his cock to be treated comfortably. He wets his finger in his mouth and sends it back into Leah's vagina. He fingers the hole rigorously, needing to stimulate its natural moisture production quickly. Her cunt responds to his finger appropriately.

Another finger joins in as the vagina stretches and moistens. He double-fingers her for less than a minute and then his entire weight is on her. He is so much taller than she is that his elbows rest above her shoulders, digging into the bed. She knows that there isn't going to be any more foreplay; she knows that he needs to get his cock into her hot place now. He needs to cum. Leah raises her knees and plants her feet on the bed. The king descends on her cunt, his broad waist flattening Leah's legs, her knees now on the bedspread to the east and west of her pussy. The king's massive cock lies on the split of her cunt, its head far above her naval. Leah closes her eyes as she realizes what the size of the king's dick is going to mean for her tiny cunt.

Her legs rise as the king lifts himself up a little. One elbow moves from the side of her head because the hand on that arm is needed to guide his dick to where it must be. The king starts adjusting his entire body, his fingers on his cock, directing it around her cunt, finding her hole, rubbing against it. Leah doesn't move at all. She knows not to. The king confirms with a finger that his cock head is on the entrance. He gives a determined dig and his head is inside. Leah closes her mouth and exhales through her nose so that the king doesn't think that he is causing her discomfort. She closes her eyes and wills her cunt to take him. The king gives her a few inches of his cock so that he has it firmly placed before returning his elbow to its original position.

Leah's hands wrap the fabric of the bed between her fingers as the king, a large mass now on top of her, sends his cock into her. He pushes it into her and splits her legs as he does, planting her knees again in their east/west locations. She can't lift herself into his cock, the king filling her completely and keeping her in place. It's his dick that lifts her off the bed slightly every time he pulls out. In, out, in, and out he moves his dick, the force moving Leah around only slightly in a small circle on the bed. Her head moves closer and closer to the head of the bed too now as the king's forward-thrusting gains as much momentum as his cock-satisfying-cunt-crunching circles. Leah no longer hides the fact that her cunt is being deliciously ripped to shreds. She lets out loud moans every time the king moves.

Because he can't get his entire dick inside her, his lower back strains. The king lifts his elbows off the bed and places his hands on it instead. His legs stretch far behind him and his toes dig into the bed as his cock makes a much more significant dive into Leah. The king has created enough reach now so that it feels like he sends his entire cock into her, his thrusts more complete. The only part of him moving is his ass as he lifts and lowers it to facilitate the powerful strokes he sends into the quivering cunt beneath him. Wetter and wetter Leah becomes, but this offers her cunt no relief from the complete drag of the king's cock on her vagina.

Closer to climax now the king places his hands on the wall behind Leah's head, above her. His toes still are digging into the bed and his legs straightening now so that he has even less control over how deep he goes, just needing as much pussy around his cock as is possible. Leah tries again to bend her knees, impossible under the king's weight. The only place for her to move her ass is down into the bed. She puts all her power into this movement, a movement that has her squeeze the king's dick so tightly with the muscles of her cunt that she yells out at the slightest attempt the king makes to free his cock from the jam. He thrusts into her hard and deep, throwing a circular twist in an effort to loosen the cunt. His attempt is unsuccessful and he has to use his mouth to ask Leah to let up her vaginal vice a little.

No sooner has she done this then the king starts to thrust deep and hard. Leah manages to will her cunt relaxed every time her pussy tenses involuntarily around the cock inside her. The king is sending himself so deeply into her now that her cunt strains against itself as it tries to process its climax. She cums in gushers and the bed moistens under her as she flows uncontrollably. The king's dick takes advantage of this free flow and starts to fuck the chambermaid as though her cunt had no end to its dark, damp depths. All Leah can do is brace herself against the king's shoulders, all the strength in her moving from every part of her body and into her hands, which she presses hard against his shoulders. Her movement is of someone wanting to push the beast off of her. The beast knows better.

The ripples in the walls of Leah's vagina fold and flex under the pleasure-filled pressure from his majesty's penis. The multiple orgasms she's having start to fuse into one long sensual explosion. The king is pleased by the familiar sounds of a satisfied woman that come from Leah. He has never fucked anyone who hasn't given him this audible confirmation that he has taken her to the limits of carnal pleasure and then pushed her over the edge. He is an extremely capable lover, not just for his strength or the size of his dick. But now that Leah is in the deep throws of an explosive orgasm, the king can take himself over that same edge.

Fire starts to fill his groin. He wraps himself around Leah and turns onto his back so that she is on top of him. Her legs are closed tight between his, the king's trunk-size legs wrapped completely around them. His hands are on her ass, her arms around his neck, and her hands in his hair at the back of his head. It feels as though the king's cock has filled her entire abdomen. She breathes hot air into his neck, the tingle from the king's chest hair against her breasts completing the circuit of her climax. The king's grip on her ass sends her cunt down onto his cock and he thrusts up at the same time. His upwards thrusting sees him lift off of the bed. Upon his collapse back on to it, half of his meat is released from Leah's cunt. Repeatedly he lifts her into the air like this, himself too. Her extended climax has her silently gasping into his neck.

The king now places his thumbs under her hips, exactly

at her waist. The eight fingers on her ass dig into the perfect butt. This grip on her mid-section means that the king can now do with Leah's cunt exactly what his cock needs. He pushes her pussy down hard so that the cock hits it in its farthest corners. Then he pushes her down towards his balls, her entire body sliding south. This move has Leah bite into the king's shoulder. He then lifts her straight up towards the ceiling, slightly, before pulling her back towards his face, her cunt sliding away from his balls towards the head of his massive cock. This complete drop, slide, lift, and pull creates a loop that the king compliments with swift thrusts up into Leah's pussy in the direction of the sky.

This is his motion, his fuck-to-cum rhythm. The movement over and around his cock completes his own circuit and he starts his steady climb towards orgasm. Leah morphs from ragdoll to a muscled Amazonian warrior as every muscle in her body tenses and releases as the king's cock digs out the depths of her pussy and extracts both her own pleasure and his. The pace of his fucking quickens now as he starts to get close to blowing. He rams her hard, and he rams her high. He holds her hard against his cock now as he stirs her cunt completely. She knots her arms around his neck and squeezes so hard that she pushes waves of pleasure from the base of his neck all the way to his cock. He starts to blow.

The roars escaping the king are loud. He pushes Leah down on his cock so that her cunt slides in the direction of his now-swollen nut-sack. His balls pulsate as they pump gallons of cum into his shaft. His dick itself seems to expand inside her pussy as it starts to fill her with white-hot wetness. She herself screams with ecstasy as her pussy soaks up the heat and gives off some of her own. Over and over, the king's cock spews into her cunt as it bangs the back of her cunt through the love potion they're mixing up inside her. Finally, the king gives her the end-thrust that sends them both into the perfect closing stages of their orgasms that has the king slump back into the bed, and Leah sheepishly slipping off to clean herself up.

CHAPTER 6

PLANTATION TEMPTATION

IT WAS THE YEAR 1863, right in the midst of the bloody Civil War. I was a slave owner's wife although I wasn't proud to admit it. We had a plantation in Mississippi. My husband was a harsh man and he treated his slaves with an iron fist. I did not agree with anything he said or did, but if I dared challenge him, he would whip me with a belt. So I kept my mouth shut unless I wanted to be treated like one of his farmhand slaves.

When my husband was away on business, I would try to treat the slaves nicely and give them good things to eat and drink. I loved all of them and they were my family. I had no children or anyone else. I was lonely and very amorous. I needed the loving of a good strong man but I didn't think I'd ever get it until I saw our slave Gus working the fields one day, his sweat running down and soaking his pants revealing a very nice looking cock against the wet cloth. I must admit my hairy quim became drenched in the hot July heat underneath my bloomers. But a lady must keep her nether regions covered or be judged not but more a wench.

My name is Chastity Somersworth but the slaves called

me Ms. Chastity or Ms. Chas. Gus got me so worked up and flushed I decided to sneak away to the natural pond and cool my hairy underparts in the cool water. My delicate woman parts were in dire need of some attention. I was known to play with my sweet cookie from time to time. I had my right hand hidden under the water playing my fuzzy muff better than a fiddle player. I was so enthralled with my naughty deeds that I failed to notice the shirtless Gus walk up. I heard Gus "ahem", clear his deep voice, and say, "Hello Ms. Chastity...I am terribly sorry to interrupt your afternoon dip. Please forgive my intrusion." I quickly dipped up to my chin in the cool water and said, "That's quite alright Gus, no harm done."

Gus and I exchanged intimate glances and our eyes caught like will happen between a gentleman and a lady from time to time. I don't know if it was the summer heat or the beads of sweat forming on Gus' dark rippled abs and biceps but before either of us had time to think, Gus was kissing me passionately. He was tonguing me hard and we both were ravaging the other in the pond. I could feel his ebony gun pressing onto my ivory thighs underwater. I looked down to see his massive black rod proudly displayed under the clear ripples of water. I put my right hand into my furry muffin and my left index finger twisted my carnation pink areola

I surprisingly let out a little girlish-sounding moan that made Gus go wild in the eyes with wanton desire and lust. He scooped me up with his big black arms and carried me to a bed of moss tucked away in the daisy field. He straddled over me, and I could see sweat forming on his brow as he prepared to enter my wet canal. He slipped slowly inside my pulsating flower inch by delicious inch. I felt my long luscious lips begin to wrap around his girth. Then they gripped him tight and snatched him deep within my tunnel. "Dick my hot cunt Gus!" I cried as he plowed my moist plantation with every inch of strength he had. He was fucking me like an alpha wolf and I was practically screaming out in the meadow like a bitch in heat. Gus flipped me over and we did it doggie style. He slapped my cotton white ass while he plunged in and out hard and furious. Gus was riding me like a tractor across the field thrusting his 9-inch trouser snake in as deep as he could, groaning like an animal and pulling out with a popping sound that drove me wild.

It had been so long since I had been made love to or fucked that it didn't take long for me to reach the nirvana state of sweet orgasmic release. Upon hearing me cum Gus was then enticed to release a powerful and tantalizing load of hot jism deep within my love canal. As Gus came, he gripped my voluptuous hips and cried a cry of needed release. He clenched his dick and I literally felt his massive gonads unload within me hosing me down with warm, sticky cock seed.

After bringing us both to an amazing climax with his fucking, I looked at his still seething black cock as it hung like a tired snake by his dark and muscular thighs. He asked me to turn over and he lifted my alabaster thighs up by his ears, and he went down onto my pussy and wallowed in it like a dog He groaned and lapped every last drop from me. I came a second time, more powerful than the first. I had never had such a wild and passionate orgasm or fucking in my life. I humped his face while he suckled my love button dry. I collapsed onto the moss and flowers relaxed and pleasured indeed.

For several years thereafter, there was not a week that passed that Gus and I didn't sneak off to our pond and meadow to partake of intimacy and lust. Gus was the love and lover of my life and I never lost an ounce of desire for his big black member from that time forward. I needed Gus and he needed me. If it hadn't been for Gus, I may have never known the true pleasures or passions of the temptation on the plantation.

CHAPTER 7

SAVING THE FAIR MAIDEN

"BRING HER TO ME AT ONCE," the King commanded to his loyal servants. The men quickly left his presence and went into the village to search for the young girl whose name they didn't know.

"There she is!" one of the soldiers shouted, pointing to the young girl in the distance.

Today was Bella's twenty-second birthday, and it was also the day she was supposed to marry King Jaffrey. When she caught sight of soldiers Bella dropped what she was doing and began running, brushing past everyone in her way.

Suddenly, two huge arms captured her and pulled her into a dark alley, away from the oncoming soldiers. Looking up at the stranger, she gasped - it was her childhood friend Adman. He and his mother had left Rome to travel to another city just before King Jaffrey took over. Although she didn't want to get him involved in her mess, Adman demanded answers.

Why was she running away from the soldiers? Had she done something wrong? His voice was laced with genuine concern as he asked.

When Bella finally explained the situation, he laughed. "We can definitely take care of that," he gave her a devious little smile. She had explained that out of all the maidens in the city the King had picked her to be his new bride. He knew that she was a virgin and had never been with anyone else before and this has persuaded him that she was the right person for him.

"You see, if you're no longer a virgin, the king will let you be. He'll find himself another virgin maiden and then you can be with anyone you choose."

Bella laughed at his suggestion but soon realized that he was serious. Thinking about it all, she too realized that this was perhaps the only solution to her problem. She knew that she didn't want to be with the king, period.

Adman led her to his house, secretly hiding her with a black veil covering her face. His house was empty; she could tell that he was a nomad. He invited her to get comfortable on his small bed, where he would soon join her.

· · ·

"Remove your attire," he said.

Bella had never done this before and felt a nervous feeling creep upon her. Was she doing the right thing? Weighing her options she decided that it would be better to sleep with Adman, her childhood friend, rather than sleep with King Jaffrey who was so much older than she was; he could literally be her father's father.

As she laid there completely naked, she felt a strange feeling. Warmness down below. Her pussy was becoming moist, and her body ached to feel Adman's body against hers.

"Just relax, you'll enjoy it," he comforted her as he stood to undress himself before her. Suddenly something caught her attention. It was a huge cock – Adman's cock. She had never seen a cock before in her life, but she'd heard from her friends about making love and so she felt a little curious as to how it would be for her.

Adman slowly lowered himself to her, parting her legs and caressing her pussy with his tongue. Bella felt an unimaginable amount of pleasure, unlike anything she'd ever felt before in her life. His tongue swept through her tender untouched folds, licking almost every inch of her pussy.

. . .

As he pleasured her down below, Bella became more and more wanton for him; her body ached to feel more of him. He increased her pleasure when he wrapped his tongue over and around her clitoris sucking it occasionally.

"Oh Adman!" she moaned bucking her pussy against his increasingly hungry caress.

Finally, he pulled away from her pussy and returned but this time, his cock made contact with her wetness. Slowly he penetrated her tight virgin pussy.

"Oh God Adman!" Bella shrieked gripping firmly unto the sheets of his bed. The force of his erection penetrating into her slit was almost too much to bear. There was a burning sensation, as Adman pressed his cock against the tight restricting muscles of her pussy.

Bella wanted to tell him to stop and a minute of more pain would have probably been her own undoing. But surprisingly Adman managed to break through the barriers with his cock, thrusting his dick deeper into her pussy, burying himself to the hilt.

Once inside her pussy, he began moving in and out of her temple of delight, stroking her walls with his massive cock. Several soft moans escaped her lips as he changed the overbearing feeling of pain and distress into a sweet wanton feeling. Bella was now ecstatic; the pain had been replaced by pleasure.

Slowly Adman began working his cock inside her massaging her breasts as he went along. Closing her eyes, Bella parted her legs further, allowing him full access into her wet pussy. Over and over, he plummeted his cock into her wetness, increasing the momentum of his thrusts as he went along.

Tiny spasms rocked through Bella's body as she found herself, quickly approaching her earthshattering climax. Adman too was thoroughly enjoying fucking her. His loud groans seemed to fill the room, as he began ramming his cock into her wetness, complimenting her on how tight she was.

Bella blushed as she, too let out several ecstatic cries. The pleasure that he was bestowing upon her with his massive cock was almost too much to bear. Bucking her pussy against his cock, she began heaving her body, meeting his thrusts halfway.

Adman increased the momentum of his thrusts, serving her with a series of long hard thrusts that sent her pussy quiver-ing. Her juices seemed to be coating his cock as he continued to penetrate her moist heat. Over and over, he buried himself inside her, until he could no longer control himself. With a loud groan, he served her with a mighty hard thrust and penetrated her core to its deepest depth.

. . .

His load of hot cum shot into her pussy as he climaxed. He continued to thrust into her pussy and soon she too let out a loud ecstatic cry as she summited her climax.

Adman soon collapsed beside her tired and spent from their moment of pleasure. "Done, you're now free from the King," he teased, planting a soft kiss on her forehead.

Bella laughed. Technically she was free from the king. He would never wed a young woman who wasn't a virgin.

ABOUT THE AUTHOR

Kellie Granier is an emerging erotica author of many erotica kinks and sub-genres. Be sure to check out other books and leave a review if this story got you hot!

Visit my blog at Kellie Granier Blog

Join my newsletter for exclusive Kellie Granier Newsletter

Sign up for Free Stories from Xplicit Press Authors

Xplicit Press Author Updates

Like Xplicit Press on Facebook

Follow Xplicit Press on Twitter

Readers: I want to expand a few of the stories to see where the characters can be explored further. If there are any of the stories that you would like to read more about again, I'd love to hear from you!

Keep In Touch
Kellie Granier
info@kelliegranier.com